A Royal Pet Problem

Adapted by Andrea Posner-Sanchez
from the script "Scrambled Pets" by Erica Rothschild

Illustrated by the Disney Storybook Art Team

A GOLDEN BOOK • NEW YORK

Sofia, James, Amber, and their friend Vivian are on the castle playground with their pets. Freedo the baboon is happily chasing a ball. Praline the peacock is trying to keep his feathers neat. Clover is eating—as usual. And an excited Crackle keeps breathing fire.

"James, your baboon keeps bumping into all the other pets," Amber complains. "We should bring them to a bigger playground—like the one at school."

"That doesn't sound like a very good idea," says Sofia. But they all agree to bring their pets to school the very next day.

The following morning, Sofia, Amber, James, and Vivian arrive at school with bigger bags than usual. But they won't have time to go to the playground until after sorcery class.

"Good morning, tiny dancers!" says Professor Popov, the dance instructor. "Zee fairies are busy giving a tour to a new student, so I vill be your sorcery substitute."

Professor Popov dances and leaps as he makes a mix-up potion and pours it on an apple and an orange. "Perfecto!" he exclaims as he cuts the fruit in half. "Zee apple is full of orange juice, and zee orange is full of apple juice! Now you try."

The professor hands out fruit to all the students. Praline and Clover lick their lips and poke their heads out of their bags.

"You can eat later," Sofia whispers nervously to them.

When the professor twirls out of the classroom, Clover and Praline can no longer resist. They rush for an apple. Crackle tries to stop them and gets dragged along. Freedo leaps onto the pile of pets, bumping into a mix-up potion along the way. The potion flies through the air—and spills on all four pets!

Poof!

Now Clover has
Crackle's dragon
body—and he can
breathe fire!

Crackle has Clover's
bunny teeth,
ears, and paws!

Praline has
Freedo's hairy
baboon arms!

And Freedo
has Praline's
peacock crest, tail,
wings, and legs!

All the students are stunned!

"Oh, this is bad!" cries Vivian. "This is really bad."

Just then, Freedo spots a ball and runs out the door. Praline chases him, yelling, "Come back here with my tail!"

"We have to get them back before the teachers see them!" James shouts.

Amber, James, and Vivian head to the door.

Sofia whispers, "Clover and Crackle, I am so sorry. I'll fix everything as soon as we catch Praline and Freedo."

Clover and Crackle are not happy.

"My nose burns, and I'm covered in scales," Clover complains.

"Well, I'm covered in fur, and these ears keep hitting me in the face!" Crackle says.

They can't wait to get back to normal, so they decide to look for Freedo and Praline, too. But Clover isn't used to flying, and Crackle isn't used to hopping!

From up in the air, Clover sees Praline and Freedo. "They're on the playground!" he reports. In all the excitement, a flame shoots out of Clover's mouth.

"See!" says Crackle. "That's what happens when I get excited."

"I'm beginning to understand that," Clover says, nervously holding on to the roof of the school.

The kids make it to the playground first.
Amber leads Praline back to the school, and
James carries Freedo.

Sofia is relieved to learn that Professor Popov hasn't returned to the classroom yet. But then she notices that Clover and Crackle are missing!

Sofia wants to ask a teacher for help, but Amber convinces her not to.

"James and I can make a new potion to put our pets back to normal while you and Vivian round up Crackle and Clover," says Amber.

Amber makes a potion right away, and James pours it on Freedo. **Poof!** But instead of making the baboon normal again, it makes him grow! And grow!

Sofia and Vivian soon return to the school with their pets. They hear a loud crash. An enormous Freedo charges down the hallway, followed by James, Amber, and Praline.

"The new potion didn't work," James says.

The kids catch up with Freedo in the gym. Unfortunately, Flora and Fauna are there with the new royal student!

Sofia steps up to explain everything to the fairies. "We brought our pets to school. We shouldn't have done it," she admits. "And then there was an accident."

"Well, two accidents, really," James adds, glancing at his giant baboon.

"Children, we have rules for a reason," says Flora.

"To keep all of you safe," says Fauna.

"And to keep giant beasts from wrecking our gymnasium," Flora adds.

Each fairy holds out a bottle of potion: one to shrink Freedo, and one to unscramble the pets.

But Freedo is having too much fun! He doesn't want to change back. Sofia has an idea. She tells Clover to use his fire to burn through the rope ties on one side of the volleyball net. Crackle uses her rabbit teeth to chew through the ropes on the other side. The net comes loose and falls on Freedo, trapping him.

The potions are poured on all the pets. **Poof!** They're back to normal.

As everyone walks home, Sofia apologizes to Clover.

"I'm just glad I'm back, baby. One hundred percent pure, twenty-four-karat Clover!" says the bunny.

"Woo-hoo!" Crackle chimes in as she happily breathes fire.